# Call the Bee Doctor!

## How Science Is Saving Honey Bees

Sandra Markle

Millbrook Press/Minneapolis

For Julie Mostly and all the children of Mockingbird Elementary School in Coppell, Texas

Acknowledgments: The author would like to thank the following people for sharing their enthusiasm and expertise: Antoinette Burnham, Maryland State Beekeepers Association, Rockville, Maryland; Dr. Robert Danka (Retired), US Department of Agriculture Honey Bee Breeding, Genetics, and Physiology Research Unit in Baton Rouge, Louisiana; Dr. Keith Delaplane, Department of Entomology, University of Georgia in Athens, Georgia; Dr. Jennifer Han, Department of Entomology at Washington State University, Pullman, Washington; Dr. Nicholas Naeger, Department of Entomology at Washington State University, Pullman, Washington; Dr. Thomas O'Shea-Wheller, Environment and Sustainability Institute, University of Exeter, Penryn, Cornwall, United Kingdom; Mark Patterson, Beekeeper for the Lord Mayor of London, London, United Kingdom; Dr. Frank Rinkevich, US Department of Agriculture Honey Bee Breeding, Genetics, and Physiology Research Unit in Baton Rouge, Louisiana.

A special thank-you to Skip Jeffery for his loving support during the creative process.



Millbrook Press™
An imprint of Lerner Publishing Group, Inc.
241 First Avenue North
Minneapolis, MN 55401 USA

Maps and diagrams by Bindy James on pp. 17, 27, and 33.

For reading levels and more information, look up this title at www.lernerbooks.com.

Designed by Emily Harris.

Main body text set in Johnston ITC Std. Typeface provided by ITC.

**Library of Congress Cataloging-in-Publication Data**

Names: Markle, Sandra, author.
Title: Call the bee doctor! : how science is saving honey bees / Sandra Markle.
Description: Minneapolis : Millbrook Press, [2025] | Series: Sandra Markle's science discoveries | Includes bibliographical references and index. | Audience: Ages 9–12 | Audience: Grades 4–6 | Summary: "Since colony collapse disorder began decimating US honey bees in 2006, scientists have been researching its causes and how to prevent it. Get an up-to-date look at what we know and how new innovations are saving honey bees"— Provided by publisher.
Identifiers: LCCN 2023053267 (print) | LCCN 2023053268 (ebook) | ISBN 9798765626795 (library binding) | ISBN 9798765638606 (epub)
Subjects: LCSH: Colony collapse disorder of honeybees—Prevention—Juvenile literature. | Honeybee—Diseases—Juvenile literature. | Bee culture—Juvenile literature.
Classification: LCC SF538.5.C65 M37 2025 (print) | LCC SF538.5.C65 (ebook) | DDC 638/.1—dc23/eng/20240221

LC record available at https://lccn.loc.gov/2023053267
LC ebook record available at https://lccn.loc.gov/2023053268

Manufactured in the United States of America
1-1010262-52010-5/8/2024

# Contents

# Case Still Not Solved!

**Millions of honey bees were vanishing from beehives around the world.** Only the queen bee, a few workers attending her, and the brood (developing young) remained. This occurred as early as 1998 in parts of Europe. Then it spread. In 2006, some beekeepers in the United States reported that they had lost as much as 90 percent of their honey bee colonies. Scientists rushed to investigate numerous commercial beekeeping sites. Although they didn't find any dead bees to examine, the scientists believed all the missing bees were dead. At that time, no one knew why this was happening. But any colony without lots of worker bees was doomed.

One day in October 2006, David Hackenberg was shocked when he took the top off one of his honey bee hives. Just three weeks earlier, the hive had been full of about thirty thousand worker bees. Now most were gone!

## Meet a Bee Colony

**queen**
1 per colony,
reproductive female

**drone**
300 to 3,000 per colony
reproductive male

**worker**
20,000 to 80,000 per colony
nonreproductive female

Honey bee colonies are made up of three types of bees that do different jobs. The queen bee mates with drones and lays eggs in the hive. The jobs a worker bee performs changes with her age: A ***janitor*** (0 to 3 days old) cleans hive cells. A ***nurse*** (3 to 11 days old) feeds larvae and new adults. An ***architect*** (12 to 17 days old) produces wax and builds new hive cells or repairs old ones. A ***forager*** (18 days old to the end of its life) finds and brings pollen and nectar to the hive. A worker bee that emerges in the fall lives through the winter (as long as 200 days) because the colony is mainly resting. But a worker bee emerging during the spring or summer lives only about 21 to 38 days because the colony is working hard.

As beekeepers struggled to recover from the 2006 losses, masses of worker bees again vanished in 2007 and 2008. More than a decade later, neither researchers nor beekeepers have fully solved the mysterious case of this honey bee disappearance—what came to be called colony collapse disorder (CCD). The good news is that while honey bee disappearances haven't stopped, the annual number of lost colonies has decreased. That's thanks to apiologists. They are the specialists—the bee doctors—who work to keep honey bees healthy. And healthy honey bees support a relationship that is critical to all living things on Earth: the honey bee–plant partnership.

# The Honey Bee–Plant Partnership

The honey bee–plant partnership depends on two things to allow bees and plants to thrive and reproduce. First, plants produce nectar (a substance to attract pollinators including honey bees) and pollen (male reproductive cells). Worker bees collect both as food for their colony. Second, honey bees spread pollen between flowers of the same kind of plant, such as blossoms on different apple trees. This enables plants to reproduce.

The pollen grains that merge with a plant's ovules must come from the same kind of plant. Luckily, honey bees often visit only one kind of plant during a single nectar-collection flight, such as different apple trees in an orchard. And one foraging honey bee visits as many as one hundred flowers during each nectar-collection flight.

Flower blossoms are often shaped to require a visiting bee to burrow inside to collect nectar. That forces the bee to pass a flower's stamen (male parts) covered with pollen. The pollen sticks to the bee's fuzzy body. Within the flower, pollen grains already sticking to a bee's body from visiting another flower brush off on the pistil (female part). Those grains grow down into the pistil and merge with the flower's ovules (female reproductive cells). Then a seed forms. Every seed the plant produces can grow into a new plant if it lands on fertile soil and receives the sunshine and water it needs.

This apple seed sprouted, and a new tree began to grow. It will need to keep growing for eight to ten years before the apple tree produces flowers that can be pollinated and grow into fruit.

A worker bee carries pollen home in baskets formed by stiff, curved hairs on its legs. It also carries nectar for the

A worker bee sucks up nectar with its strawlike mouthpart called a proboscis. Back at the hive, it passes this liquid—now a mixture of nectar and special digestives juices produced by the bee's body—through its proboscis to a younger worker bee that will store it in the comb.

colony in its two stomachs where this liquid mixes with its digestive juices. The worker passes the nectar from one of its stomachs off to another bee in the hive. The nectar in its other stomach is its own food supply.

The bee receiving the pre-honey (nectar plus digestive juices) adds its own digestive juices and pumps this liquid into a cell in the hive's wax comb (wall of wax cells). Then lots of worker bees fan their wings over that section of the comb. This increases airflow over the mixture in the cells. Nectar straight from the flower is as much as 80 percent water. The airflow causes some of the water to evaporate (move into the air). But doing this once isn't enough. Another bee sucks up the liquid, adding more digestive juices, and repeats the process. This process happens five or more times. And, little by little, the liquid becomes the thick, sugar-rich honey that bees store to eat later when nectar is not available.

The bees also use the plant's pollen for food. Each returning forager backs into one of the hive's empty cells and uses its feet to comb pollen off its body and pack it into the cell. Other workers chew the pollen, mixing it with a little honey. That turns the pollen into beebread, a high-protein food bees need to stay strong and healthy.

The partnership between bees and plants is key to both. Without plants producing nectar and pollen, bees wouldn't have food. And without bees visiting the flowers to collect nectar and pollen, many plants wouldn't be able to reproduce. Imagine how plants dying without new plants growing could impact the Earth!

# Prime Suspects

**The honey bee–plant partnership benefits another group—people!** The Food and Agricultural Organization of the United Nations estimates that as much as one-third of the world's food production depends on honey bees doing their part. In fact, honey bees are so important some people manage and care for colonies of honey bees the way others tend cattle, chickens, or other animals. They are commercial beekeepers. And when they were suffering losses of many of their bee colonies, it was the apiologist's detective work that turned up the prime suspects for what caused worker bees to disappear.

At first, though, they had a lot of possibilities. These included aliens, cell phones, and audio recorders. Researchers quickly ruled out aliens as illogical. And they tested cell phones and audio recorders by putting some in beehives and playing noises on them. When the noise had no effect on the bees, these devices were ruled out too. But apiologists found enough evidence to consider four possible causes of CCD: pesticides, poor nutrition, parasites, and pathogens.

1. ***Pesticides***. Many farmers spray chemicals on their fields to destroy insects that harm their crops. But those chemicals also kill honey bees and other beneficial insects.

**2. *Poor nutrition.*** Most farmers rent bee colonies from commercial beekeepers to pollinate their crops. The bees are shut inside their hives and loaded onto a truck for transport. Once they reach the pollination site, the hives are unloaded and reopened. If the bees arrive before the plants begin blooming, the bees are fed sugar syrup. Eating only sugar syrup gives bees a lot of energy, but it is a poor diet that could weaken them or shorten their already short lives.

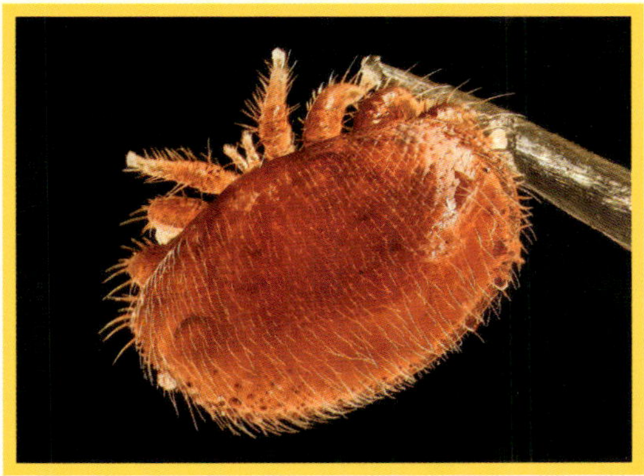

**3. *Parasites.*** These organisms live in or on other living things, including bees. And they live at the expense of their host. A Varroa mite (*left*) is a parasite that weakens or even kills honey bees.

**4. *Pathogens.*** Viruses, bacteria, and fungi infect bees and can kill them The deformed wing virus causes honey bees to mature without fully formed wings (*right*). Their wings are too small and weak for them to fly.

# Clues Are Key

**At first, the bee doctors were focused on determining which prime suspect was causing CCD.** But not one of the four suspected causes could be linked to every colony that collapsed. Some bee colonies survived despite having Varroa mites. Other colonies survived when some worker bees had a pathogen, such as deformed wing virus. And some colonies recovered after pesticides were sprayed nearby or after the bees were weakened from spending an extended period on a sugar syrup diet.

The bee doctors realized that all the prime suspects—either acting alone or in combination with others—were affecting bee health. They concluded there wasn't just one cause of CCD, which meant varied solutions would be required. Those would have to work for commercial beekeepers who transported lots of colonies long distances to pollinate crops. So, what could be done to help keep honey bee colonies healthy?

A beekeeper examines his bees, checking their health.

## Family Split

A honey bee colony normally swarms in the springtime when the number of worker bees rapidly increases in preparation for nectar collecting. Swarming means the colony splits in two. About half the worker bees remain with the old queen, and the rest leave with a new queen the colony produced.

This swarming behavior helped beekeepers recover somewhat from CCD losses because in the springtime—before they needed the bees to work for them—they could split the hives themselves. To do that, beekeepers moved about half the worker bees to a new hive, leaving behind the queen, drones (reproductive males), and other workers. Next, the beekeepers gave the newly formed colony a new queen purchased from commercial beekeepers who specialize in raising queen bees. But even better, during this controlled doubling, the new colony could be given a queen especially bred to have certain desirable traits. That meant that the brood of bees the new queen produced would also have those desirable traits, such as being resistant to certain pathogens. Since a worker bee's life span is only about twenty-one to thirty-eight days during the spring and summer, it never took long for all the bees in the new colony to share the queen's special traits.

If allowed to swarm naturally, the worker bees suck up honey from their home hive to carry along as a temporary food supply for the new colony. That keeps the colony going until the bees find a sheltered spot, and some workers start building a wax comb while others forage to bring home nectar and pollen.

# Prescription 1:
# Vaccinate Queens

## One disease harming honey bees is American foulbrood (AFB).

It's caused by a pathogen—*Paenibacillus larvae* (PEENA-buh-sill-lus LAR-vee) bacteria. The bacteria spread by producing tiny seedlike parts called spores. These get on flower pollen and are carried home when the pollen sticks to worker bees. The bacteria don't affect adult honey bees, but this pathogen is deadly to larvae (developing young). Once a larva dies, its body turns to slime. Seeing slime in a hive's comb is how beekeepers tell a colony is infected with AFB. They can feed the bees antibiotics—medicine that keeps the spores from sprouting. But once the antibiotic is gone, the spores can sprout again. So, the disease never really goes away after a colony is infected. And if AFB bacteria is in one hive, the beekeeper's gloves or equipment can spread it to colonies in other hives.

This cotton swab is covered with slime—the remains of a dead bee larva. The bacteria in the larva's gut multiplied rapidly, killing the developing bee.

In the past, the only way to stop the spread of AFB was to destroy the infected colony and burn its hive. Then, in 2018, Dalial Freitak and Heli Salmela at the University of Helsinki in Helsinki, Finland, created an AFB vaccine.

Nurse bees feed honey bee larvae (*shown*) beebread. It contains minerals and vitamins they need to develop into healthy adult bees.

A queen honey bee (*blue dot*) deposits an egg in a cell. A queen produces as many as 2,500 eggs daily. Each egg contains vitellogenin (ve-TEL-loh-gen-in), a substance similar to the white part of a chicken egg. Researchers don't yet know how, but vitellogenin helps move particles of the AFB bacterium from the vaccinated queen into her eggs.

In the past, researchers believed honey bees lacked an immune system, so they could not be vaccinated. Then further studies showed honey bees do have an immune system, but it's very different from a human's. A human's immune system produces antibodies—special proteins that can destroy or block disease-causing pathogens. Once vaccinated (exposed to a substance to stimulate immunity), it will produce those antibodies any time it is exposed to the same pathogen. A honey bee's immune system responds to any pathogen by triggering the production of melanin. In humans, melanin is the pigment that colors skin, hair, and eyes. But in honey bees, melanin encases and destroys pathogens. Freitak and Salmela discovered a queen bee could be fed chopped-up AFB bacteria and become vaccinated against this pathogen. But how could they vaccinate an entire bee colony?

Specialized commercial beekeepers focus on raising queens to sell to beekeepers managing bees for crop pollination and honey production. The queen raisers start with healthy colonies known for good honey production. Then they give each colony synthetic (man-made) queen cups. These simulate the larger cells worker bees construct in the hive to raise larva to become queens. The queen lays her eggs in the cups, or the queen raiser inserts newly hatched larva into the cups. Then the workers care for the developing queen larvae exclusively feeding them royal jelly. This special substance, which is produced by workers, is what larvae need to become reproductive females—queens. Beekeepers remove the developing queens from the hive before they emerge as adults to prevent the active queen from destroying them. The new queens are moved into their own small beehives. Upon emerging, the queens take a mating flight, mating with free-flying drones from nearby colonies. After the queens return to their hives, they are captured and shipped to commercial beekeepers.

Apiologists tested different methods to vaccinate the bees and learned a vaccinated queen bee could pass on her immunity. So, they could mix chopped-up AFB-causing bacteria into queen candy—soft, pasty sugar a queen bee feeds on while in her travel cage on her way to join a colony. Then the vaccinated queen would pass along her AFB immunity to every egg she produced. Larvae hatching from those eggs immediately reacted to AFB pathogens by producing melanin. And they survived.

Since beekeepers usually replace a colony's queen as often as every six months, the vaccination effect is proving to last her lifetime. And the US Department of Agriculture found vaccinated bees produced honey safe for humans to eat. So, on January 4, 2023, the Department of Agriculture officially approved commercial beekeepers using AFB-vaccinated queen bees for their colonies.

The newly vaccinated queen is surrounded by her colony's attending worker bees. With her abdomen down inside a cell, she deposits an egg from which a vaccinated larva will hatch.

## Prescription 2:
# Give Food Supplements

**Varroa mites are honey bee parasites.** When a Varroa mite gets on an adult bee, it uses its mouthparts to slice open small holes in the bee's exoskeleton (rigid body covering that provides both support and protection). Then it eats the soft tissue on the inside, and the bee dies. Sometimes a Varroa mite feeds on a sick bee. Then the mite can spread the virus it picked up whenever it moves on and feeds on another bee.

Varroa mites also spread easily from one colony to another. A mite may jump onto a wandering drone that drifts into an infested hive from another colony and then moves on to a healthy colony. Or a mite may hop onto a worker bee that comes to steal honey. The worker bee then ends up taking home both food and a Varroa mite, launching an infestation. Beekeepers can even spread these parasites, if mites are present, among worker bees being split to start a new colony.

A Varroa mite's scientific name is *Varroa destructor.* This cousin of ticks is so harmful it destroys whole colonies.

# Bee vs. Mite Life Cycle

Any Varroa mite that is feeding on an adult bee is a female ready to produce eggs. The mite's life cycle goes along with the honey bee's life cycle.

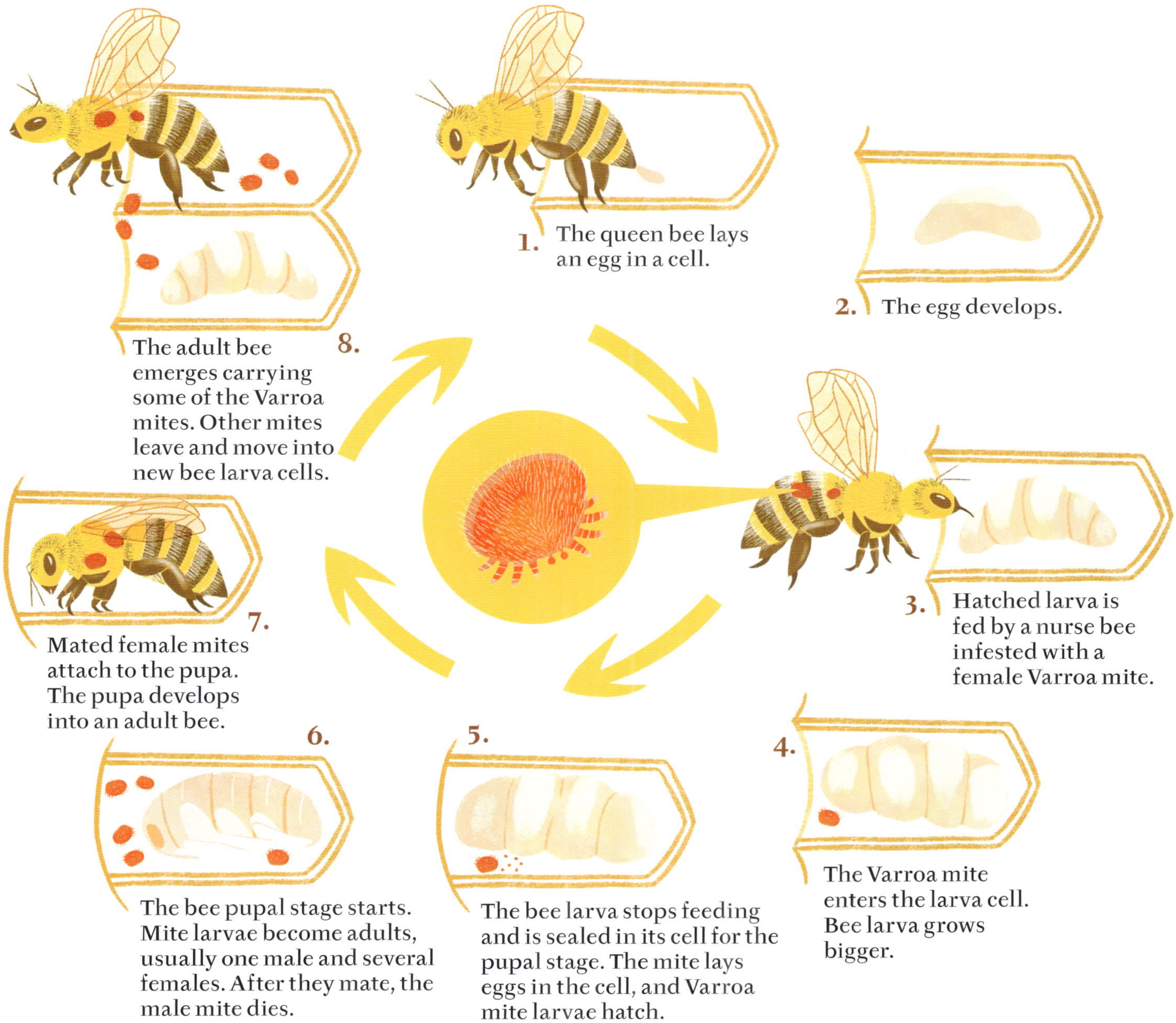

Varroa mites weaken their adult bee hosts as they feed. So, the weakened bees can't fly to visit as many flowers to collect pollen and nectar for the colony. Varroa mites also spread viruses that affect larvae and adult bees. Both deformed wing virus and acute bee paralysis virus limit or make it impossible for the infected adult bee to fly. Larvae infected with sacbrood virus die before they become adults.

Nicholas Naeger was studying how honey bees learn which flowers are in bloom when CCD became a crisis in 2006. While trying to figure out how to help, he discovered honey bees were as attracted to puddles on decaying wood as they were to flower nectar. He thought about how people take aspirin and other over-the-counter drugs when they don't feel well. Naeger said, "I wondered if infected honey bees could be self-medicating by sipping what's in that puddle water?" He also wondered if what was in the water that pooled on decaying wood could be used to help make worker bees stronger and healthier.

Each bee is sipping the water with its proboscis.

Nicholas Naeger holds a *Fomes* (FOH-mez) mushroom, and Jennifer Han holds a *Ganoderma* (GA-nuh-dur-muh) mushroom, two of the kinds of fungi they tested. The plastic bottles of bee food supplements contain extracts from each of these test fungi.

Naeger figured the puddle water had to include some kind of fungus. Mushrooms are the most visible part of fungi. But, like a plant's flowers, mushrooms are the reproductive part of a fungus and are not around for long. The rootlike part of fungi, the mycelium, is long-lived. That's the part of some fungi people began using as medicine in ancient Greece.

Naeger wanted to investigate whether eating an extract made from the mycelium of fungi that break down wood could help honey bees stay strong even if infected by viruses spread by Varroa mites. So, he joined forces with Jennifer Han, who was already working on how fungi could help honey bees. They assembled a research team to test Naeger's idea.

To start, Naeger and Han chose six bee colonies to test in their laboratory. Three of the colonies showed signs that diseases were affecting their health. The other three appeared in good health. That gave them a mix of sick and healthy bees, which was important. If all the bees died or all the bees lived after treatment, it would be impossible to judge whether receiving food supplemented with the fungal extract affected bee health. Naeger said, "We needed an intermediate level of sickness to see effects." So, without the fungal extract, the bees had a fifty-fifty chance of surviving or of becoming ill and dying from mite-transmitted infections within the test time period.

A beekeeper uses a shaker box to collect bees from hive frames.

Once the colonies were chosen, some worker bees from each colony were transferred into a beekeeper shaker box. There, the bees from all the different colonies were allowed to mingle for a day. That way, infected bees exposed the healthy bees to whatever viruses they might have.

**1.** The bees in the shaker box are misted with water to keep them from flying and stinging.

**2.** After misting, the bees are scooped out of the shaker box one-quarter cup at a time.

**3.** Each scoop of bees is dumped into a plastic cup. Then it is sealed shut.

Naeger said, "Next, we divided up that big, mixed-up [honey bee] population into little cages." The cages were plastic cups.

Han said, "I estimated there were 100 to 150 bees in each little cage. . . . And there were enough bees to fill 108 cups."

The team created two different control groups from the 108 cages. Every scientific investigation needs control groups as well as test groups. The control groups are provided conditions exactly as the subjects would normally experience. Then, comparing the results in the control group with those in the test groups makes it possible to see if what happened in the test was due to what was changed. Twelve cages were fed watered-down honey—similar to what bees normally eat in their hives. Another twelve cages received sugar syrup—what honey bees are fed while being transported to work at different pollination sites and when blooming plants are not available. None of these bees received any food supplements. The remaining eighty-four cages were divided into seven test groups—each made up of twelve cages of bees. All these test groups were fed sugar syrup. But each test group received a different supplement added to this food. The supplements varied as this testing process was repeated and the team ran test after test on different groups of bees.

4. The researchers placed the bee food at the top of each cup cage. And the bees immediately went to work building a wax comb to store this food.

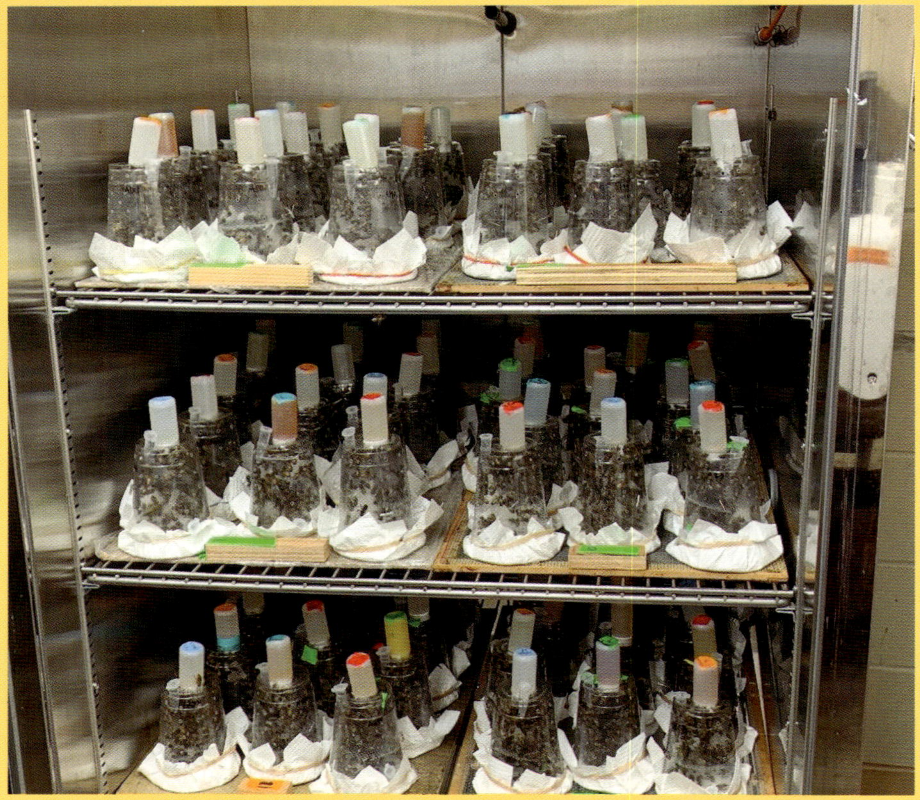

The incubator maintained 35 to 45 percent humidity and a temperature of 89.6°F (32°C). This was slightly cooler and less humid than the climate inside a typical beehive. But those conditions allowed for the additional humidity and heat created by the bees being close together inside the cup cages.

For the duration of every testing cycle, the research team placed all the cages (control and test groups) in an incubator, so the environment inside each was identical and ideal for the bees. The team fed the bees for three weeks. They chose the length of this test period because it was within the two-to-six-week spring and summer life span of healthy worker bees. At the end of three weeks, Naeger and Han counted how many bees survived in each control group and each test group.

Naeger said, "We tested around a dozen species [of fungi]. The best performers were *Ganoderma lucidum* (GA-nuh-dur-muh LOO-si-dum) and *Ganoderma resinaceum* (GA-nuh-dur-muh REH-zin-ays-um)." Both come from species of reishi (REE-she) mushrooms.

Han added, "We think these reishi extracts are replacing or supplementing the nectar's chemicals, which helps the bees being fed sugar syrup boost their immune system and helps them fight off a variety of health problems."

After completing their series of laboratory tests, Naeger and Han worked with their team on field tests to see if the reishi food supplement they developed would help bees in working colonies. The team created a special frame to use in each field-tested hive. They plan to do more testing to determine how often a working bee colony should be fed the food supplement for the best results. Han said, "Anytime the bees are drinking sugar syrup, there is no reason not to make that healthier for them—make it like *super food*."

Naeger inserts a feeder frame into the hive. This frame will be filled with sugar syrup and the food supplement.

The food supplement still needs to be approved by the Association of American Feed Control Officials because it's a kind of animal food. It must also be approved by the US Food and Drug Administration since some of what bees eat while producing honey ends up in the honey people eat. Naeger and Han are already working on getting these approvals so the food supplement can become available to commercial beekeepers in the United States and then worldwide to help honey bees.

# Prescription 3: Modify Genes

## What would help honey bees even more than being strong enough to survive living with Varroa mites in their colony?

***The answer is limiting the number of Varroa mites in honey bee colonies.***

Varroa mite populations stay small enough not to be a problem for Asian honey bees—*Apis cerana* (A-puhs sir-AN-uh)—which are native to parts of Asia. That is because the worker bees tending the colony's developing brood detect the presence of Varroa mites. Researchers believe the bees do this by sensing odors a bee pupa gives off when it is damaged by Varroa mites. Then the worker bees remove the infested pupa from the hive. That limits the number of weak and diseased adults in the colony. It also gets rid of the young Varroa mites before they can reproduce. For Asian honey bees, sensing and removing of Varroa mites is a genetic trait—the behavior is inherited and exhibited by every Asian honey bee colony. Researchers call this hygienic behavior.

This is an Asian honey bee colony. These bees produce less honey than western honey bee colonies. And Asian honey bee colonies often abandon hives supplied by people. Instead, they build their homes in other places, such as this clay jar.

## Selected Countries with Varroa Mite Populations*

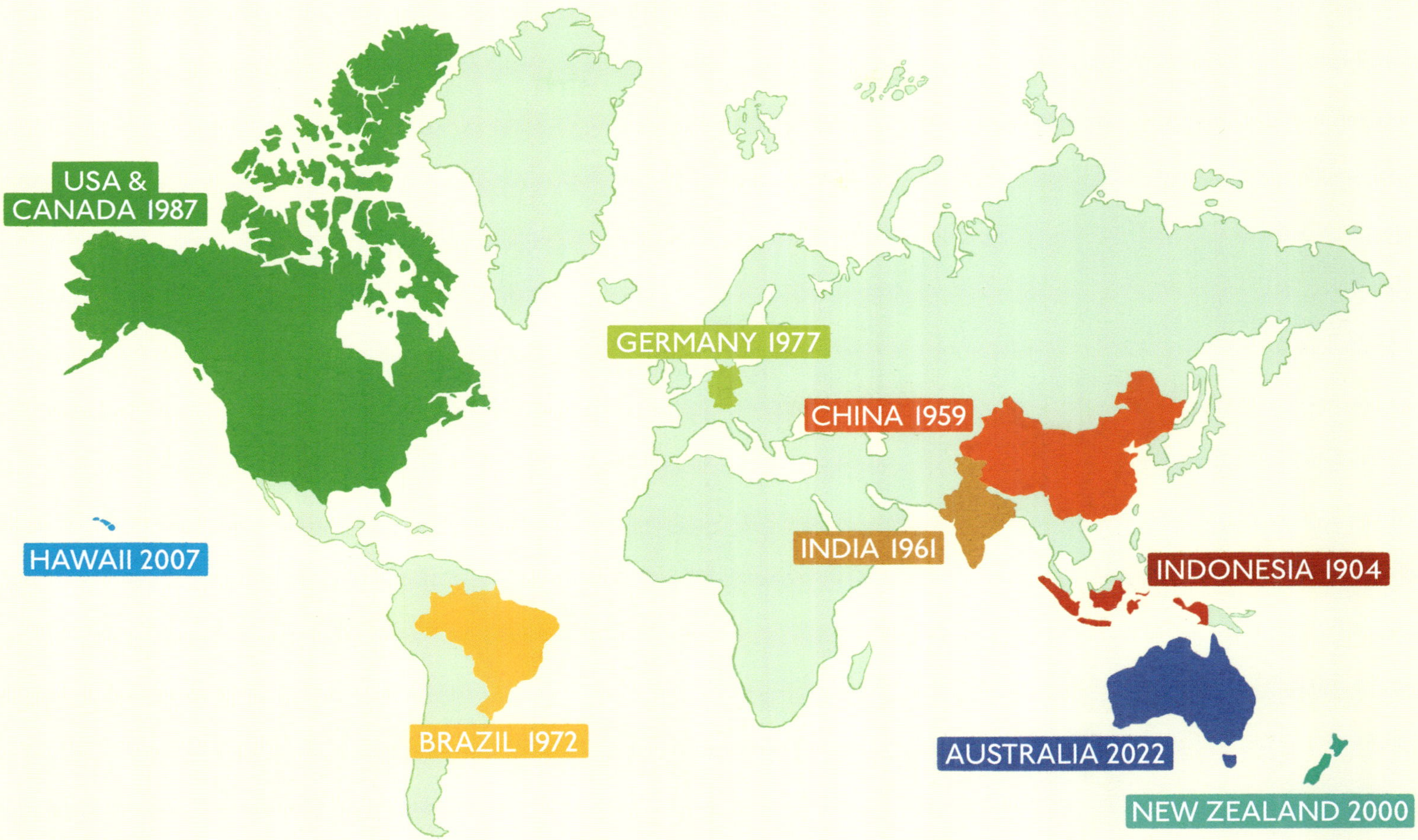


*Check the dates and countries to follow the spread of Varroa mites around the world.

Unfortunately, western honey bees—*Apis mellifera* (A-puhs muh-LIF-er-uh)—that are common everywhere outside Asia don't normally exhibit hygienic behavior.

Scientists believe Asian honey bees may have developed hygienic behavior because they have a long history of being attacked by Varroa mites. These mites more recently spread to areas outside Asia as an invasive species. But there may be hope for the western honey bee colonies.

When the worker bees tending the brood sense the presence of Varroa mites on a pupa, the pupa is removed from the hive.

In 1997 John Harbo and Jeffrey Harris were conducting research at the US Department of Agriculture–Agricultural Research Service Honey Bee Breeding, Genetics, and Physiology Laboratory in Baton Rouge, Louisiana. They discovered that some western honey bee colonies did remove pupae infested with Varroa mites. Those bees maintained low Varroa mite levels in their colonies. Harbo and Harris called this behavior suppression of mite reproduction. But had it happened by chance or were the bees seeking mite-infested pupae to remove?

The Baton Rouge laboratory team tested a number of honey bee colonies that were infested with Varroa mites. They counted the number of mites in each colony at the beginning and end of a seventy-day test. While most colonies had much higher numbers of mites at the end of the study, a small number had fewer than at the beginning. From 1997 through 2008, the team conducted more rounds of tests to identify what behaviors the bees were using to keep Varroa mite populations low. And they observed whether those behaviors were being passed on to the next generation.

During their research, the team found that a colony with worker bees that removed Varroa-infested pupae had a smaller Varroa mite population. Before 2007, no scientific study had been able to determine how bees managed to control the number of Varroa mites in their colony. They simply named the phenomena to describe the end result—suppression of mite reproduction. Now, they had observed the bees in action detecting and removing any mite-infested pupae. So, they changed the name of the bees exhibiting this behavior to Varroa sensitive hygiene (VSH). In other words, the bees sensed the mite-infested pupae and cleaned them out.

Robert Danka, at that time the research leader at the Baton Rouge Laboratory, said, "The discovery of the Varroa sensitive hygiene trait being inherited in western honey bees was absolutely a watershed moment in the whole history of trying to find bees that are genetically resistant to Varroa mites." He added with a laugh, "It was *exciting*!" But there was still much to be done to make honey bees with the VSH trait available to commercial beekeepers.

To produce honey bees that could be counted on to inherit the VSH trait, the Baton Rouge laboratory team collected newly emerged queens from colonies that strongly exhibited the VSH trait. These queens were artificially inseminated with sperm (male reproductive cells) from drones of other colonies exhibiting the VSH trait. Then the queens laid eggs that hatched and grew into VSH trait bees.

Garrett Dodds was the lead technician for the team. Although queen bees are bigger than worker bees, he needed a steady hand and tiny tools to accomplish his task. Through Dodds's efforts, enough VSH trait queens hatched that they were offered to commercial beekeepers.

The tube gently holds a VSH trait queen bee while she is artificially inseminated with sperm cells collected from a VSH trait drone.

Almond trees need honey bees to pollinate their blooms. These beehives are home to just a few of the 2.5 million bee colonies California almond orchard owners rent from commercial beekeepers each year to pollinate their crops—about 80 percent of the world's almonds.

There quickly proved to be a *big* problem with the VSH trait honey bee stock. Frank Rinkevich is a research entomologist—someone who studies insects—with the Baton Rouge laboratory team. He noted that the original VSH bees had very little variety in their gene pool. He said, "It had smaller adult bee populations and less brood. Because when the VSH behavior turns on and the bees sense Varroa mites, they remove most of the pupae [even those not infested]. So that was kind of a detrimental trait, causing the colony to have fewer workers. And [with fewer workers] they didn't produce a lot of honey."

The solution was to let the VSH trait honey bees go a bit wild. During the 2008 to 2009 beekeeping season and again during the 2009 to 2010 season, the Baton Rouge laboratory team began a series of testing periods to improve VSH trait honey bees. They collaborated with Merrimack Valley Apiaries in Billerica, Massachusetts, which managed about twenty thousand honey bee colonies. The Merrimack Valley Apiaries split some colonies to produce queenless colonies with about seven thousand

## A Year in the Life of a Traveling Honey Bee Colony

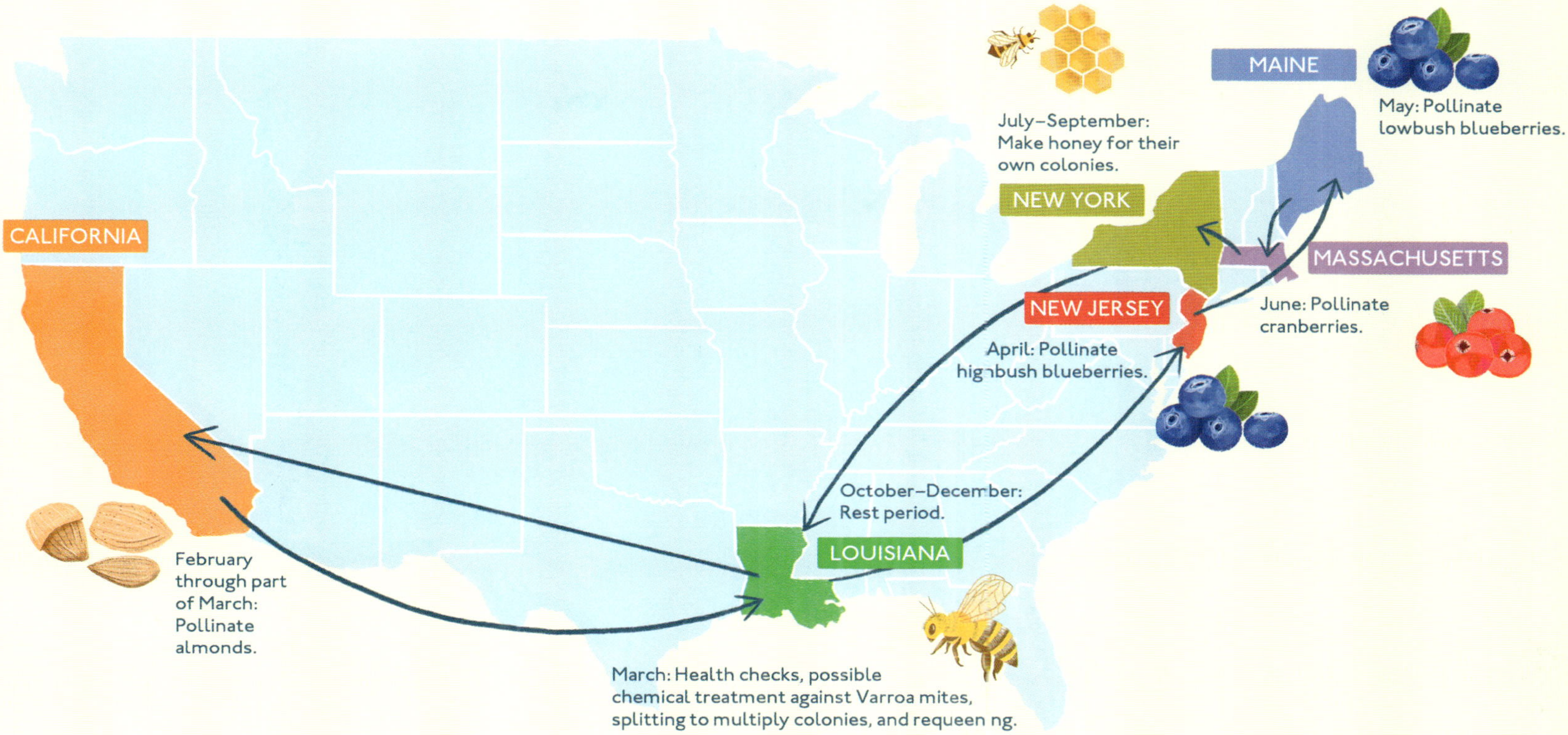


**During a year of pollinating crops in the United States, commercial honey bee colonies are regularly transported an average of 8,100 miles (13,036 km). Honey bees don't just pollinate these crops. It's estimated that honey bees pollinate around 135 kinds of fruits, nuts, and vegetables grown in the United States each year.**

worker bees and drones. The company's beekeepers gave some of those queenless colonies standard commercial stock queens. Others were given Russian honey bee queens. These are a subspecies of western honey bees that originally came from the Primorsky Krai region of Russia. They tolerated Varroa mites enough to remain good honey producers, which meant they were also good crop pollinators. Other colonies were given outcrossed VSH trait queens—laboratory-raised VSH trait queens that were allowed to fly and mate naturally with drones from commercial bee colonies.

The results at the end of the beekeeping season were what the team had hoped for. The colonies with outcrossed queens had larger populations and produced more honey than previously recorded by pure VSH trait colonies. They also had fewer Varroa mites than the regular commercial stock or Russian honey bee colonies, so they still exhibited the VSH trait.

Next, in 2010, the Baton Rouge laboratory team launched a second testing period. They collaborated with Merrimack Valley Apiaries again. But this time, they also worked with Adee Honey Farms in Bruce, South Dakota, and Lamb's Honey Farm in Jasper, Texas. The goal of this test was to tweak the genetic makeup of the queen bees so the worker bees they produced both exhibited the VSH trait and produced a lot of honey. So, during each beekeeping season that followed, they included commercial stock colonies (the control group) and outcrossed VSH trait queen colonies (the test group) in their studies. And they added outcrossed-outcrossed queen colonies, which are colonies descended from the best outcrossed queen colonies from the first test period. These queens were also allowed to fly and mate with commercial stock drones. During this second testing period, all the outcrossed queen colonies and outcrossed-outcrossed queen colonies exhibited the desired traits.

In 2011 the Baton Rouge laboratory team began to refer to the outcrossed-outcrossed queen colonies as Pol-line honey bees. Danka explained, "This name was created by Tom Glenn, a California queen breeder with whom we worked extensively. The name relates to the selection process, in which we bred with the best-performing bees after the colonies were used to pollinate almonds in California, and apples, blueberries, and cranberries in the northeastern US. So, Glenn suggested naming them 'pollination line' [Pol-line] of Varroa–resistant

When honey bees return to their hives at night, commercial beekeepers seal them inside and transport them to the next pollination sites. Some transport the hives on semitrucks. Others use smaller trucks. After arriving at the next site, the beekeepers open the hive so the bees can pollinate the crops.

bees." The best-performing colonies from this group became the founders of the genetic line officially called Pol-line stock honey bees in a 2015 scientific publication.

The third and final test period was designed to test the new Pol-line bee stock's performance in migratory commercial beekeeping during the 2017 to 2018 season. The Baton Rouge laboratory team compared stationary bee colonies (ones that remain in one location to pollinate crops) to colonies that are moved across the country to pollinate different crops.

The more honey the bee colony produced, the more the hive's weight increased—sometimes the increase was as much as 100 pounds (45 kg).

The team checked each colony in May, June, September, December, and February. They examined the queen, noted the size and health of the worker bee population, and looked for Varroa mites in the hive. Thomas O'Shea-Wheller, who led the monitoring team, reported, "When we got to the point [in the commercial beekeeping season] where honey harvesting occurred, we measured the yields from the different colonies. And we did that by weighing each colony's hive on a giant scale." The study showed that in each of the migratory beekeeping groups, the Pol-line bee colonies produced about as much honey as standard commercial bee colonies. The Pol-line bee colonies also maintained larger worker bee populations while keeping levels of Varroa mite infestation low—often with fewer than half as many mites as the commercial colonies. It was time to make queens with these genetic qualities widely available.

Since 2015 the Baton Rouge laboratory team had collaborated with a nonprofit bee health organization and a private beekeeper. With the support of this group, they established a breeding program in a remote area near Hilo, Hawaii. There, all queen bees were allowed to fly and mate naturally with drones in the area. A number of different kinds of honey bees lived around the Hilo site so the mated queens weren't pure Pol-line stock. They were outcrossed Pol-line stock, which the team named Hilo honey bees. The exact genetic makeup of these queens is not critical. Testing is proving that Hilo queens are passing on the desired genetic qualities for maintaining large worker bee populations, good honey production, and resistance to Varroa mites.

In 2023 Rinkevich said, "While Varroa mites quickly evolve resistance to miticides [chemicals used to kill mites], they have not evolved to escape genetic Varroa sensitive hygiene. Hopefully, distributing these desirable traits in western honey bees will get to a situation like *Apis cerana* [Asian honey bees] where the bees tolerate the mite, and it doesn't cause colonies to die off."

These bees are drinking honey from wax honeycomb cells. Honey supplies a bee with carbohydrates for energy, and minerals, vitamins, and enzymes to stay healthy.

These worker bees are on guard duty. They are positioned around their hive's entrance and ready to attack and drive away any intruder. But guard bees can't protect against climate change.

# Bee Doctors Still on Call

**When colony collapse disorder began affecting honey bees around the world, bee doctors responded to the urgent call for help.** While some colonies still collapse each year, the losses are no longer a crisis. Vaccinating queen bees against AFB bacteria helps colonies raise generation after generation of healthy worker bees. A new bee food supplement helps bees stay strong enough to withstand some viruses. And Varroa mite–resistant Pol-line stock and Hilo honey bee queens help commercial beekeepers maintain colonies with healthy worker populations for pollination and honey production.

But while the situation for honey bees has improved, bee doctors continue working to help honey bees overcome diseases and pests. And a new threat is affecting honey bee colonies with the potential to cause a more serious impact in the future. That threat is climate change.

This honey bee gathers pollen and nectar from a cherry blossom.

Climate change is affecting a key part of the bee-plant partnership around the world. The event is called the nectar flow. It happens during the time of year when lots of flowers are blooming, so plants are producing lots of pollen and nectar. Bees only make honey when workers bring home more nectar than is immediately needed to feed the colony. And that mainly happens during the nectar flow. In many places, including regions in the United States, the nectar flow used to happen twice a year. For example, in parts of the northeastern United States, springtime meant lots of trees and spring flowers blooming. Then, in the fall, many wildflowers bloomed and a second nectar flow happened. Due to recent changes in the global climate, though, nearly everywhere there is only one seasonal period when lots of plants are blooming at the same time. Worse, the timing of this event has changed.

A beekeeper scrapes off the wax caps to harvest the stored honey on one frame of a colony's hive. The beekeeper must leave enough full frames for the colony to feed on when plants aren't blooming.

A honey bee colony naturally begins to prepare for the spring nectar flow each year following its winter rest period. As the weather warms up, the queen produces lots of eggs. That brood matures, increasing the number of foraging workers from as few as fifteen thousand to forty thousand or more. Outside the hive, the weather continues to warm, and frequent rains help plants grow and develop nectar-producing flower buds.

But in recent times, global climate change is altering when the weather warms up to start plants blooming. In some areas, the spring nectar flow is starting as much as a month earlier. That is before the colony's worker bee population is at full force. So, bees are producing less honey. Fewer worker bees also means fewer flowers are being pollinated, which causes fewer seeds to be produced. Then there are fewer new plants to bloom and produce nectar in the following year. Year after year as the nectar flow shrinks, the impact on honey bee colonies and the bee-plant partnership increases.

In 2013 a wildfire in California's Stanislaus National Forest burned 257,314 acres (104,131 ha), destroying most plants in the area. Studies of other burned forests show it may take up to eighty years for this area to fully recover.

In 2019 heavy spring rains in Knocknamuckley in Northern Ireland badly damaged the blossoms on the trees in this apple orchard.

Climate change is also increasing droughts in some areas. That lack of rainfall prevents plant growth. And it causes many of the area's plants to die and dry out, which can fuel wildfires that wipe out more growing plants. Then those areas may have few to no plants contributing to the nectar flow.

Warmer air in other areas produce more rainstorms with heavier rainfall. Honey bees can't fly in heavy rain to collect pollen and nectar. Rain can also wash away the flowers' pollen and nectar.

Charlie Brandt (*above*) inspects the bees on one frame from a White House honey bee hive. In 2009, while working as a carpenter at the White House, Brandt told Michelle Obama, then the First Lady, about his beekeeping hobby. The Obamas had beehives placed on the South Lawn. Bees have been at the White House ever since, supplying honey to the White House kitchen.

A garden in Bryant Park in New York City (*below*) provides spring and summer blooms for the honey bee colonies in the park's hives and spotlights the value of these insect members of the community.

Who knows what innovative prescriptions bee doctors will discover in the future to help honey bees cope with the effects of climate change? Meanwhile, we can be bee doctor assistants by supporting bees living in our areas. Be willing to live with some insect pests to avoid the use of pesticide sprays in your community. Support cities maintai ning green spaces for trees and native wildflowers. If your home has a garden or a place to put a flowerpot, find out what you can grow in your area that will provide nectar for bees because every bit helps. We need to work together to keep the honey bee–plant partnership buzzing. After all, the best treatment for keeping our planet healthy is to . . .

**SAVE THE HONEY BEES!**

# A Note from Sandra Markle

When I researched my book *The Case of the Vanishing Honeybees*, which was published in 2013, the future for honey bee colonies was grim. Only breeding honey bee queens then splitting worker bee populations and adding a new queen to make one colony into two kept commercial beekeeping going—and with it the honey bee–plant partnership. In fact, I ended that book saying that the future looked grim for honey bees. So, when I learned about the development of a way to vaccinate honey bees against American foulbrood, I was excited. I needed to know more about that vaccine. And I wanted to find out what else apiologists had come up with—or were working on—to help bees survive. What I discovered blew me away. That led me to track down and interview creative, innovative, hardworking, and dedicated scientists that are truly bee doctors. The prescriptions they've developed have made such a difference that I was able to pack this story full of hope for honey bees to have a successful future. That's sweet news for all of us!

## Those Amazing Honey Bees!

- A honey bee worker beats her wings about two hundred times per second. That's what makes her buzz and lets her fly as fast as about 15 miles (24 km) per hour.
- During a worker bee's lifetime (about thirty-eight days), she produces an average of just one-twelfth of a teaspoon of honey. Since it takes twenty-four teaspoons to fill a half cup, imagine how many bees must work to produce a half cup of honey.
- When a worker bee finds a good nectar source, she returns to her hive to tell other workers. She communicates by walking in loops and shaking her body. That tells others what direction to fly and about how far they need to travel.
- Bees produce wax and, without any training or blueprints, workers build perfect six-sided tubelike cells. The worker bees slightly angle the cells up, so the honey they produce and store there won't spill out. Once a cell is full of honey, they cap it with more wax.

# Glossary

**American foulbrood (AFB):** a honey bee disease caused by *Paenibacillus larvae* bacteria that attacks bee larvae, kills them, and turns their bodies to slime

**apiologist:** a person who studies bees and honey-making

**artificial insemination:** injecting male reproductive cells into a female to produce young

**brood:** the developing young bees in a colony

**colony collapse disorder (CCD):** when an unknown combination of factors cause so many worker bees to abandon the hive that the colony dies

**commercial beekeeping:** managing bee colonies as livestock to pollinate agricultural crops or to provide honey for sale

**drone bee:** a male bee that mates with any newly emerged queen bee

**fungus:** a plantlike living thing that, unlike a plant, cannot make its own food. It feeds off another living thing. Types of fungi include mushrooms, yeasts, and bread molds.

**immunity:** being able to resist a particular disease

**melanin:** the substance a honey bee's body produces as an immune response to engulf and trap pathogens preventing them from causing it harm

**nectar:** a sweet liquid produced by flowers to attract bees for pollination

**outcross:** the transfer of genetic material from one individual to another genetically different individual. The goal is to develop offspring with better traits.

**parasite:** a living thing that lives in or on another living thing and gains what it needs to live at the other's expense

**pathogen:** a bacteria, virus, or fungus that can harm a living thing's health

**pollination:** when pollen is moved from the male part of a flower to the female part of a flower enabling the plant to produce fruit and seeds

**queen bee:** a female bee that is able to produce offspring for the colony

**royal jelly:** a special substance workers produce and feed to larvae so they develop into queens

**stock:** a group of living things that is genetically enough alike that offspring produced have the same traits

**swarming:** when a honey bee colony has two queens, one leaves, and some of the colony's worker bees go with her. Beekeepers use this behavior to split colonies and add a queen to be with the workers that are queenless.

**vaccine:** a substance used to stimulate a future immune response to a specific disease-causing pathogen

**Varroa mite:** a tiny relative of a tick that attaches itself to a honey bee and lives by sucking the honeybee's body fluids. This mite may also inject disease-causing viruses into its bee host.

**vitellogenin:** a part of a honey bee's egg thought to help the embryo develop. Scientists believe a vaccinated queen bee's AFB immunity is passed with the vitellogenin to each egg she produces.

**worker bee:** a female bee that is unable to produce offspring. Depending on her age, a worker bee performs different jobs for the colony.

## Source Notes

18 Nicholas Naeger, telephone interview with the author, November 8, 2022.

21 Naeger.

22 Naeger.

22 Jennifer Han, telephone interview with the author, November 8, 2022.

24 Naeger, interview.

24 Han, interview.

25 Han.

30 Robert Danka, telephone interview with the author, December 2, 2022.

32 Frank Rinkevich, telephone interview with the author, November 18, 2022.

34 Danka, interview.

36 Thomas O'Shea-Wheller, telephone interview with the author, November 22, 2022.

37 Rinkevich, interview.

## Find Out More

Check out these books and websites to discover even more:

Beesponsible
https://www.beesponsible.com/do/bee-gardening/
This site is packed with information for gardening with honey bees in mind. Click on the US map to discover types of bee-friendly plants that grow well in your area.

Fleming, Candace. *Honeybee: The Busy Life of* Apis Mellifera. New York: Neal Porter Books, 2020. The book is a beautifully illustrated exploration of the life of the type of bee the scientists are trying to save. This is the kind of bee commercial beekeepers tend and the world counts on for pollinating food crops.

How Do Bees Make Honey?
https://www.youtube.com/watch?v=A4YIpGQiD3w
This is a fun to watch, easy-to-follow presentation on both pollination and how honey bees produce honey.

Markle, Sandra. *The Case of the Vanishing Honeybees: A Scientific Mystery*. Minneapolis: Millbrook Press, 2013. Investigate the events that led up to *Call the Bee Doctor*.

Milner, Charlotte. *The Bee Book*. New York: DK, 2018. An illustrated view of the bee's everyday life, it shares an overview of the many different kinds of bees in the world.

World of Honeybees
https://www.wholekidsfoundation.org/bees-and-our-food
With close-up photos, videos, and activities, this site includes opportunities to learn about honey bees and beekeeping.

# Index



# Photo Credits

Image Credits: LazingBee/Getty Images, p. 1; © Ingo Arndt/Minden Pictures, AP Photo/Jimmy May, p. 4, p. 5 (top); Wataru Yanagita/Getty Images, p. 6 (bottom); Nigel Cattlin/Alamy, p. 6 (bottom); Michael T. Bentley, PhD, pp. 6, 12, 37; Reed Kaestner/Getty Images, p. 8; © Chris and Tilde Stuart/Minden Pictures, p. 9 (top); © 2020 Images/Alamy, p. 9 (middle); N. L. Naeger, pp. 9 (bottom), 20, 21, 22 (all), 23, 24, 25; Johner Images/Alamy, p. 10; Samuel Ray/Alamy, p. 11; Avalon.red/Alamy, p. 13 (top); Paul Starosta/Getty Images, p. 13 (bottom); Keith S. Delaplane/Professor of Entomology, University of Georgia, p. 15; © Mark Moffett/Minden Pictures, p. 16; Ingo Arndt/naturepl.com, p. 18–19; GUNTIMA SUWANNAPONG, p. 26; Don Johnston_IH/Alamy, p. 28; Science History Images/Alamy, p. 28 (inset); Paolo Negri/Getty Images, pp. 30–31; Barbara Rich/Getty Images, p. 32; Dr Thomas O'Shea-Wheller, pp. 34, 36; xalanx/Getty Images, p. 35; Michael T. Bentley, PhD, p. 37; Paul Weston/Alamy, p. 38; Grant Heilman Photography/Alamy, p. 40; Juan Rodriguez Pazos/Alamy, p. 41; CALFIRE/Alamy, p. 42 (top); David Hunter/Alamy, p. 42 (bottom); White House Photo/Alamy, p. 43 (left); Patti McConville/Alamy, p. 43 (right); Skip Jeffrey Photography, p. 44; Peter Cripps/Alamy, p. 45.

Cover: Werner Lippert/500px/Getty Images.